Griffin's Someday

by Becky Nguyen
illustrations by Daniela Camacho

Griffin's Someday
First published in 2016 by Hartfield Press
Text copyright © 2016 Becky Nguyen
Illustrations copyright © 2016 Daniela Camacho
ISBN-13: 978-0-9982750-0-0
ISBN-10: 0-9982750-0-X
First Edition: November 2016
10 9 8 7 6 5 4 3 2 1

HARTFIELD PRESS

Griffin's Someday

by Becky Nguyen

illustrations by Daniela Camacho

HARTFIELD PRESS

Someday, I'll be an astronaut soaring in space

or an Olympian athlete competing in a race.

I'll bounce around in a big, fluffy suit

or outrun my opponent and have a "hoot!"

Someday, I'll be a Pro Football player

or lead a town as the greatest mayor.

I'll run many yards and score touchdowns

or help solve problems all around.

Someday, I'll sing under bright stage lights

or run a bakery shop, with icing just right.

I'll twirl and dance to the musical sounds

or bake a cake for a customer downtown.

Someday, I'll be a doctor and give great care

or a firefighter on duty, without a dare.

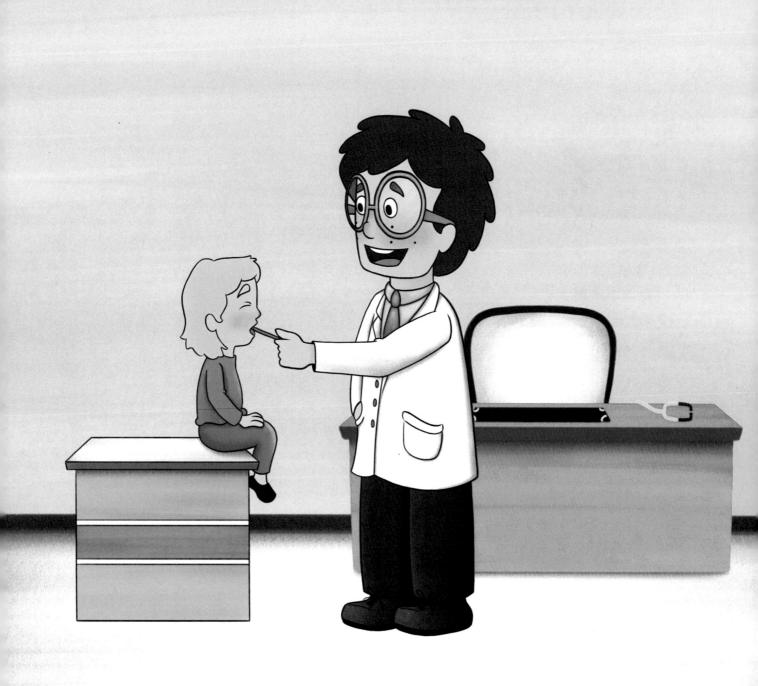

I'll listen and soothe your worries and pain

or tackle a fire, even in the rain.

Someday, I'll build giant buildings and bridges

or be a teacher, who reads and writes digits.

I'll estimate and measure to be precise

or look at naughty students and say, "Think twice."

The sound of the school bell gave me a fright.

Mrs. Bailey asked if I was all right.

My cheeks lifted and eyes filled with glee.

Someday will come. Just you wait and see!

This book is dedicated to Mom and Dad, for giving me the world. - B.N.

Made in the USA
San Bernardino, CA
01 December 2016